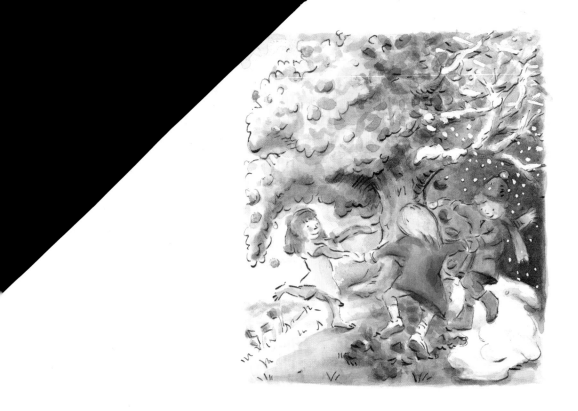

For the children and the trees

Text and illustrations copyright © Laurence Anholt 1992

First published in Great Britain in 1992 by
Frances Lincoln Limited, Apollo Works
5 Charlton Kings Road, London NW5 2SB

British Library Cataloguing in Publication Data
available on request

ISBN 0-7112-0680-5 hardback

Set in Joanna Regular by F.M.T. Graphics Limited
Printed and bound in Hong Kong

1 3 5 7 9 8 6 4 2

THE Forgotten Forest

Laurence Anholt

FRANCES LINCOLN

A long time ago, but not so far away, there was a country that was covered by trees.

People used to say that a squirrel could leap from branch to branch, right from one coast to the other.

The great forests were often full of the sounds of
children laughing – and sometimes the chopping of axes

as trees were cleared to make way for houses.
There were so many trees it didn't seem to matter.

And the trees could not complain – even when whole forests were cleared to make way for towns.

Year in, year out. A leaf for every brick.

Until one day there was only a single forest left.

One small forest like an island
in the endless, noisy sea of the city.

And everyone had forgotten it was there.
No one had time to think about trees any more.

Everyone had forgotten – except the children.

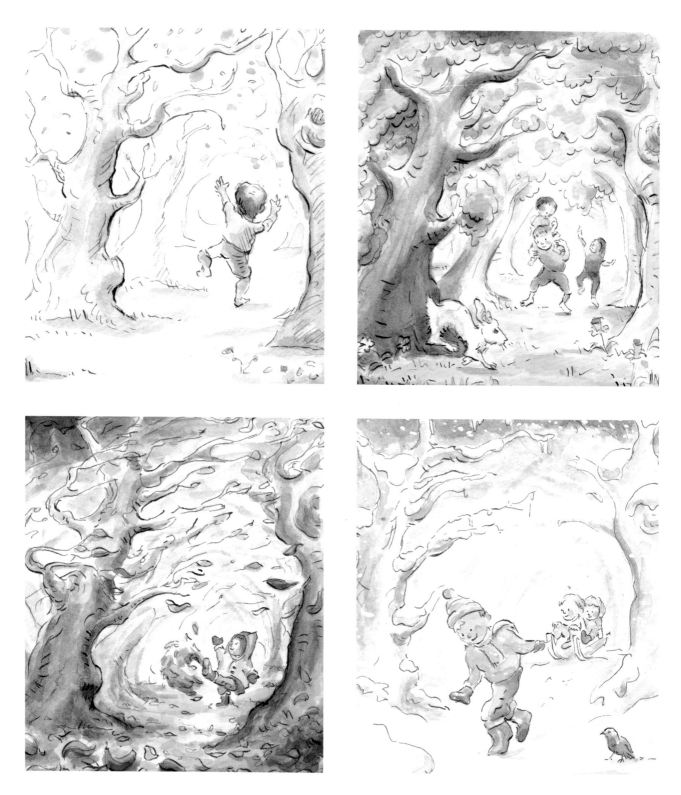

Through all the seasons of the year

the children played in the forgotten forest.

Then one day a terrible thing happened. A man hung a notice on the forest fence. It said: BUILDING STARTS TOMORROW.

If the trees could talk they would have cried out then.

The builders opened the gate into the forest . . .
and were amazed by what they found. It was all
so peaceful, so silent.

But listen! There *was* a noise – at first a whispering in the leaves, then a sighing, then a crying. Louder and louder until it sounded as though the whole forest was weeping.

And there in the very centre of the forest were all the children.
It was the children crying for the trees.

"Come on!" shouted a man. "We have seen enough."
"Yes!" said the builders. "We must start work straightaway."

But it was not the trees they pulled down –

it was the fence around them.

The children danced with joy – but the work had only just begun. "We will plant new trees!" the builders shouted. "A tree for every child. Trees in every street. Who will help? Will you help?"

And in the forgotten forest there was a whispering, then a chuckling. Louder and louder until it sounded as though the whole forest was laughing.
Or was it just the children playing in the trees?